To Cliff, Nigel, Arlene, Eric, and Effie.

American edition published in 2018 by Andersen Press USA,
an imprint of Andersen Press Ltd.
www.andersenpressusa.com

First published in Great Britain
in 2018 by Andersen Press Ltd.,
20 Vauxhall Bridge Road, London SW1V 2SA.

Distributed in the United States and Canada by
Lerner Publishing Group, Inc.
241 First Avenue North
Minneapolis, MN 55401 USA
For reading levels and more information, look up this title
at www.lernerbooks.com.

Printed and bound in China.

Library of Congress Cataloging-in-Publication Data Available
ISBN: 978-1-5415-3564-0
eBook ISBN: 978-1-5415-3565-7

1-TOPPAN-6/5/18

An
ANTY-WAR
Story

(Ant)Tony Ross

Andersen Press USA

At last, the ants found the perfect place

and so they built their Antworld on the spot.

The ants worked hard. Antworld was a happy place,
where lots of little ants were born.

One little ant was different: he had a name.
He did not know WHY he had a name, and neither
did the other ants. His name was Douglas.

Douglas watched the other ants form a beautiful
line. All day, they hurried past carrying food.
"Why do you do that?" asked Douglas.

"So we can eat it over here," was the reply.
"Why don't you eat it over there?" asked Douglas.
"Let's not talk about it!" was the reply.

Douglas thought that was a fine answer. Now he knew
what he wanted to do with his life. He wanted to
fit in, to carry food, and be in the beautiful line.

But as he grew bigger, nobody asked Douglas to do
anything at all. At last, he went to the Chief Ant.
"I want to fit in," he said.

The Chief Ant examined his papers and his lists.
"Uhhhhh ... no!" he replied. "We have you down
for other things. Important things."

"You are a big ant. You have a big head and
big teeth." Douglas felt proud and very special.
"We have you down as a soldier."

"I will gladly be a soldier," said Douglas.
"What is a soldier? Will I carry food and be
in the beautiful line?"

The Chief Ant waved his papers at Douglas.
"You will not carry food, you will carry a rifle."
Douglas felt sad. "But you will have a uniform."

Douglas was worried, but he promised he would do his best. "What must a soldier do?" he asked. "He must defend Antworld," replied the Chief Ant.

So Douglas proudly put on his uniform, glad that
his big head and big teeth would make Antworld
a safer place for the little ants.

With his rifle on his shoulder, Douglas joined
the beautiful line of soldiers as they marched
up and down and the little ants waved flags.

The band played. Douglas felt happy to be a
soldier, and to be in a beautiful line, and to
keep the little ants safe ...

The end.